David Baron, Art Lyon

Michael Heisler: letters

Brian Wood:
Original series & collected edition covers

KU-229-104

⑥

殴りつける場所は、骨盤、太もも、脇腹など。

Jim Lee, Editorial Director ▸ John Nee, VP – Business Development ▸ Scott Dunbier, Executive Editor
Kristy Quinn, Assistant Editor ▸ Robbin Brosterman, Senior Art Director ▸ Ed Roeder, Art Director
Paul Levitz, President & Publisher ▸ Georg Brewer, VP–Design & Retail Product Development
Richard Bruning, Senior VP–Creative Director ▸ Patrick Caldon, Senior VP–Finance & Operations
Chris Caramalis, VP–Finance ▸ Terri Cunningham, VP–Managing Editor ▸ Alison Gill, VP–Manufacturing
Rich Johnson, VP–Book Trade Sales ▸ Hank Kanalz, VP–General Manager, WildStorm
Lillian Laserson, Senior VP & General Counsel ▸ David McKillips, VP–Advertising & Custom Publishing
Gregory Noveck, Senior VP– Creative Affairs ▸ Cheryl Rubin, Senior VP–Brand Management
Bob Wayne, VP–Sales & Marketing

ARE YOU ON THE **GLOBAL FREQUENCY?**

ARE YOU ON THE GLOBAL FREQUENCY.

LONDON BOROUGH OF HACKNEY

3 8040 01182 5629

GLOBAL FREQUENCY created by: Warren Ellis

Collected edition design: Larry Berry

GLOBAL FREQUENCY: DETONATION RADIO, published by WildStorm Productions. 888 Prospect St. #240, La Jolla, CA 92037. Compilation, cover and new material copyright © 2005 DC Comics. All Rights Reserved. GLOBAL FREQUENCY is ™ Warren Ellis. Originally published in single magazine form as GLOBAL FREQUENCY #7-12 copyright © 2003, 2004 Warren Ellis and DC Comics. WildStorm Signature Series is a trademark of DC Comics. The stories, characters, and incidents mentioned in this magazine are entirely fictional. Printed on recyclable paper. WildStorm does not read or accept unsolicited submissions of ideas, stories or artwork. Printed in Canada.

DC Comics, a Warner Bros. Entertainment Company.

DETONATION

BERLIN: TODAY

MR. GERRARD.

MY NAME IS MIRANDA ZERO. AND YOU'RE ON THE GLOBAL FREQUENCY.

STAND DOWN.

IT'S A DUBIOUS PLEASURE TO MEET YOU, MS. ZERO. I ADMIRE YOUR WORK, BUT YOUR PRESENCE TENDS TO IMPLY TROUBLE.

GLOBAL FREQUENCY IS PRIMARILY A RESCUE ORGANIZATION. MAY I ASK WHO NEEDS RESCUING TODAY?

YOU.

OKAY. EVERYONE INSIDE THE KILLZONE IS ON THE FREQUENCY OR A COP IN PLAINCLOTHES.

NO REACTION FROM THEIR POSITIONS, SO WE'RE GOOD TO GO.

MY PEOPLE ARE DRIVING THE CARS BY REMOTE CONTROL FROM INSIDE THE VAN.

AND NO, YOU CAN'T WATCH.

SHAME, REALLY. THIS NEXT BIT WILL BE FUN.

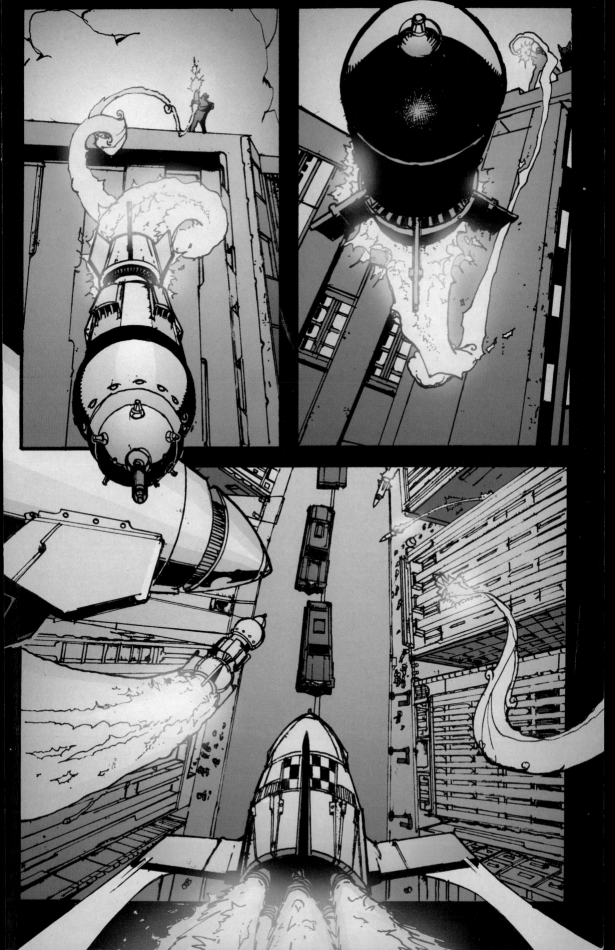

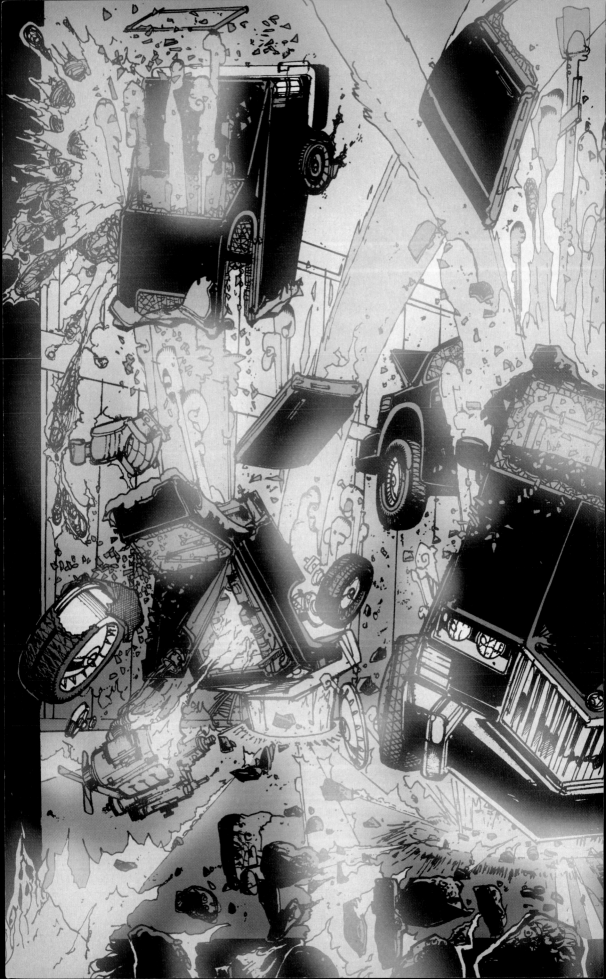

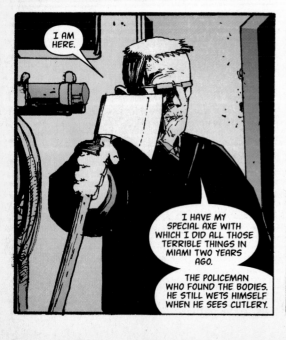

THIS IS LAU. WEST SIDE OF FLOOR THIRTY-FIVE.

HEAVY RECONSTRUCTION THERE--PARTS OF THAT AREA DON'T EVEN HAVE POWER.

I KNOW.

SILENT CALL

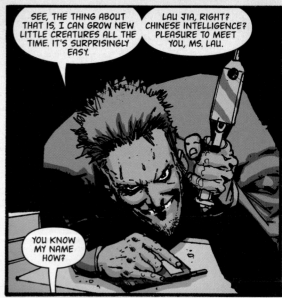

WE EVEN KNOW ABOUT THE NUCLEAR DEVICE YOU INTENDED TO EXPLODE OVER LONDON, PARKED AT HAMBURG AIRPORT.

PUT THE GUN DOWN. MIRANDA ZERO IS EAGER TO MEET WITH YOU. SHE'S EVEN READ YOUR E-BOOK.

YOU KNOW ABOUT THE DEVICE? NO, YOU DON'T.

IF YOU KNEW ABOUT THE DEVICE, YOU'D KNOW IT'S ON A PLANE THAT'S ALREADY IN THE AIR.

AND THE DEVICE IS TRIGGERED BY A CODE TEXTED TO IT FROM A SATELLITE-ENABLED MOBILE PHONE.

IT'LL STILL BE OVER GERMAN SOIL, RIGHT NOW.

IT'S A DIRTY DEVICE. IMAGINE WHAT IT'D RAIN DOWN ON GERMANY.

NOT PERFECT, BECAUSE OF COURSE I WANTED IT TO BE PERCEIVED AS A GERMAN ATTACK ON LONDON, BUT PLANS RARELY SURVIVE REALITY.

IMAGINE ALL THE LITTLE HOUSES UNDERNEATH IT. ALL THE LITTLE CHILDREN.

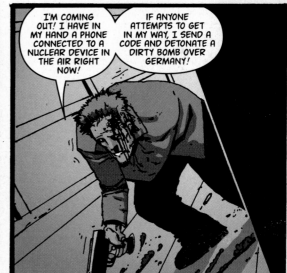

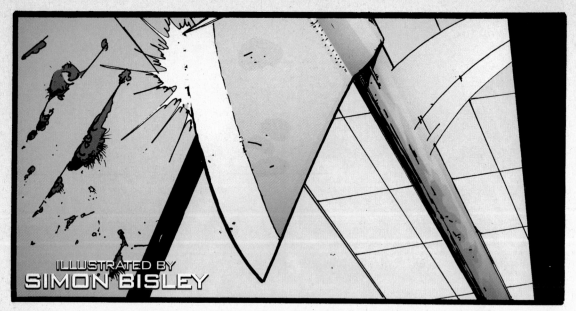

ILLUSTRATED BY
SIMON BISLEY

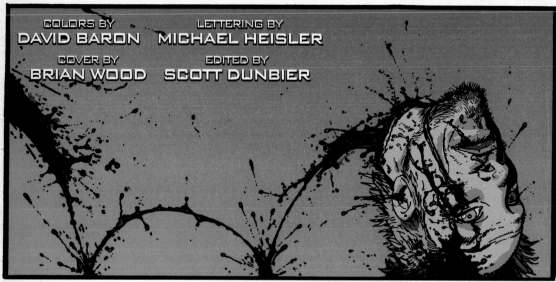

COLORS BY
DAVID BARON

LETTERING BY
MICHAEL HEISLER

COVER BY
BRIAN WOOD

EDITED BY
SCOTT DUNBIER

LAU HAD HER PHONE ON THE ENTIRE TIME. ALEPH HEARD YOUR MOBILE PHONE EXPLODE.

CREATED AND WRITTEN BY
WARREN ELLIS

AND SHE TOLD YOU THAT YOU WERE NOT LEAVING THE ROOM.

the End

THIS IS ALEPH IN GLOBAL FREQUENCY CENTRAL TO ALL LOS ANGELES AREA UNITS.

MIRANDA ZERO HAS BEEN UNREACHABLE FOR EXACTLY TEN MINUTES.

EMERGENCY RECOVERY PROCEDURE BEGINS NOW.

11.31 AM

MARK TRAN, YOU'RE ON THE GLOBAL FREQUENCY--

ALREADY GOT THE EMERGENCY KIT. WHERE AM I HEADED?

THE SUTTON HOTEL, WEST HOLLYWOOD. WE NEED YOU TO SEAL HER ROOM THERE.

I'M FIVE MINUTES AWAY BY AIR. AM I GOING TO HAVE SPACE TO LAND?

TALKING TO LAPD ABOUT CLEARING AND SEALING THE STREET NOW.

I'M IN THE AIR IN ONE MINUTE. GUYS, I'M TESTING THE SOLOSOAR MYSELF, PRESS CONFERENCE WILL HAVE TO WAIT--

THIS IS WINSTON CROFT.

YOU'RE OUT OF RETIREMENT AND ON THE GLOBAL FREQUENCY, MR. CROFT.

A HELICOPTER WILL BE LANDING OUTSIDE YOUR HOME IN AROUND TEN MINUTES.

WHAT'S GOING ON?

MIRANDA ZERO HAS DISAPPEARED. WE NEED A DETECTIVE.

YOU'RE THE BEST DETECTIVE WE KNOW, AND THE ONLY ONE IN THE LOS ANGELES AREA.

WE KNOW YOU WANTED TO BE LEFT ALONE--

WELL, YES. OBVIOUSLY I'M APPALLED.

BUT, YOU KNOW...I THINK I CAN FORCE MYSELF TO WORK AGAIN.

11.35 AM

WELL? THE SILENCE IS MOST RUDE.

YOU MAY AS WELL JUST HAVE YOUR HIRED RETARD WITH THE GUN COME IN AND SHOOT ME.

HOW'S HIS FACE, BY THE WAY?

UNPRETTY. LUCKILY, AS YOU NOTE, HE HAS THE BRAIN AND NERVOUS SYSTEM OF COMMON LIVESTOCK.

IN A DAY OR TWO, HE MAY ACTUALLY NOTICE WHAT YOU DID TO HIS NOSE.

AND THEN HE'LL BE GLAD HE SHOT YOU.

PERHAPS, IN A WEEK OR SO, WE'LL LET HIM COME BACK AND PLAY WITH YOUR BODY.

IF YOUR LITTLE HELPERS HAVEN'T FOUND YOUR CORPSE BY THEN, OF COURSE.

OR.

YOU COULD GIVE ME THE CODES.

YOU WILL LIVE TO FIGHT ANOTHER DAY. PERHAPS REBUILD YOUR ORGANIZATION, IN A FEW YEARS. WHO KNOWS?

BUT FOR NOW, WE WANT YOU OFF THE PLAYING FIELD.

YEAH. THERE'S LOCKS ON SOME OF THIS, BUT WE'RE TALKING PRE-OP RESEARCH, ANESTHETICS AND THE LIKE.

AND NEW SURGICAL PROCEDURES. BIOREACTORS, FOR CULTURING REPLACEMENT SKIN CELLS AND THE LIKE.

LET ME BREAK SOME OF THESE LOCKS.

BE QUICK. I CAN HEAR SOMETHING.

I'M APPROACHING ONE OF THE SECONDARY VESTIBULES. I COULD USE THERMAL SATELLITE TAKE, IF YOU HAVE IT...

TRYING TO RETASK A SAT NOW. YOU'LL HAVE TO MAKE DO WITH THE BLUEPRINT UNTIL THEN.

ALL THE DIRECTION SIGNS HAVE BEEN TAKEN DOWN.

SOME KIND OF SECONDARY HALL BEHIND THE LOBBY. I HEAR VOICES.

GOING IN.

ILLUSTRATED BY LEE BERMEJO

COLORS BY
DAVID BARON
LETTERING BY
MICHAEL HEISLER
COVER BY
BRIAN WOOD
EDITED BY
SCOTT DUNBIER

CREATED AND WRITTEN BY WARREN ELLIS

END

SUPERVIOLENCE

AAAOWWW!

OW OW
OW

GGGGHHHHH

THAT'S IT. GO THROUGH YOUR BIOFEEDBACK PROCESS. SEE IF YOU CAN SHUT *THAT* PAIN NOW, M. WELLFARE.

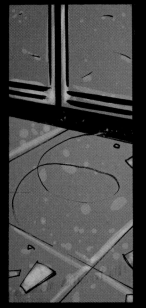

MY
GIFT

ENOUGH.

NOT ENOUGH.

UNTIL I'M EATING YOUR GODDAMN HEART

NOT WHAT I MEANT.

MY ENGLISH IS NOT SO GOOD SOMETIMES.

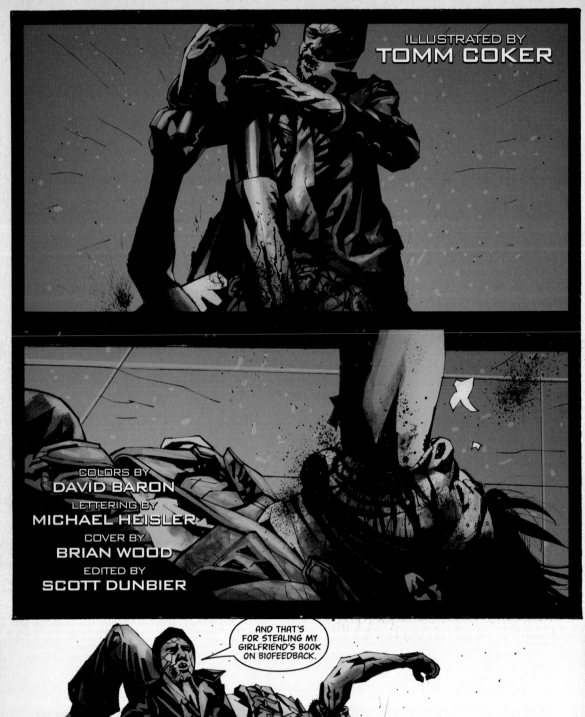

ILLUSTRATED BY
TOMM COKER

COLORS BY
DAVID BARON
LETTERING BY
MICHAEL HEISLER
COVER BY
BRIAN WOOD
EDITED BY
SCOTT DUNBIER

AND THAT'S FOR STEALING MY GIRLFRIEND'S BOOK ON BIOFEEDBACK.

CREATED AND WRITTEN BY
WARREN ELLIS

END

GIMME THAT.

YOU'RE THE GLOBAL FREQUENCY WOMAN.

YOU PREDICTED THE METHANE BUILD-UP IN THAT RWANDAN LAKE AND GOT THE VILLAGERS OUT BEFORE THE EXPLOSION.

YEAH. WHAT I NEED IS SOMEONE TO BE THAT CENTRAL WHEEL, CONNECTING UP ALL THE POINTS ON THE FREQUENCY.

WHAT'S YOUR NAME?

MIRANDA ZERO.

NO, REALLY. WHAT'S YOUR NAME?

THAT'S THE ONLY ONE YOU'RE GETTING.

IS THAT, LIKE, YOUR SPECIAL GLOBAL FREQUENCY NAME? DO I GET ONE?

CALLSIGN ALEPH.

A?

YOU'VE NOT READ BORGES?

DOES BORGES WRITE BUFFY EPISODES?

NO.

THEN I'VE NOT READ BORGES.

WHOA.

JAPAN
SATELLITE:AQUA
SENSOR:MODIS
08/213/97/05

GF SAT RETASK

IN HIS SHORT STORIES, HE TALKS ABOUT A THING CALLED AN ALEPH; THE POINT FROM WHICH YOU CAN SEE ALL OTHER POINTS IN THE UNIVERSE.

THAT'S WHAT YOU'LL BE DOING. SEEING EVERYTHING AND TYING IT ALL TOGETHER.

IS IT DANGEROUS?

I HAVE A LOCATION SET UP FOR YOU. VERY SAFE. YOU'LL NEVER HAVE TO GO INTO THE FIELD.

THE PAY IS VARIABLE?

IT'LL VARY FROM GOOD TO EXCELLENT. BUT YOU MIGHT NEVER HAVE THE TIME TO SPEND IT.

YOU'VE HEARD OF INTERNET SHOPPING, RIGHT?

GOT IT.

IT'S TAKEN FOUR YEARS, BUT WE'VE GOT IT.

WE'VE FINALLY NAILED DOWN THE LOCATION OF GLOBAL FREQUENCY CENTRAL OPERATIONS.

AND IT'S BEEN RIGHT UNDER OUR NOSES ALL ALONG.

MID MANHATTAN

TODAY:

NEW!

ALEPH, THIS IS
MIRANDA ZERO, AND
I'M AFRAID YOU'RE
ON THE GLOBAL
FREQUENCY.

AND NOT
IN A GOOD
WAY.

GLOBAL
FREQUENCY CENTRAL
OPERATIONS HAS BEEN
COMPROMISED.

UM...
HELLO?

3:19

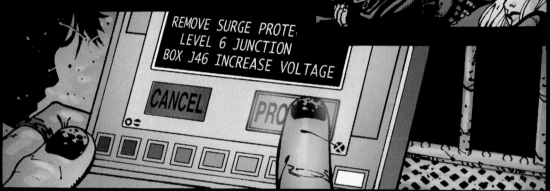

REMOVE SURGE PROTE
LEVEL 6 JUNCTION
BOX J46 INCREASE VOLTAGE

CANCEL   PRO

THE
HELL?

GET
OFF THE
GROUND--

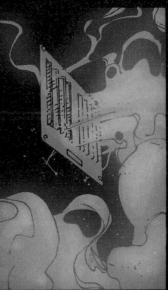

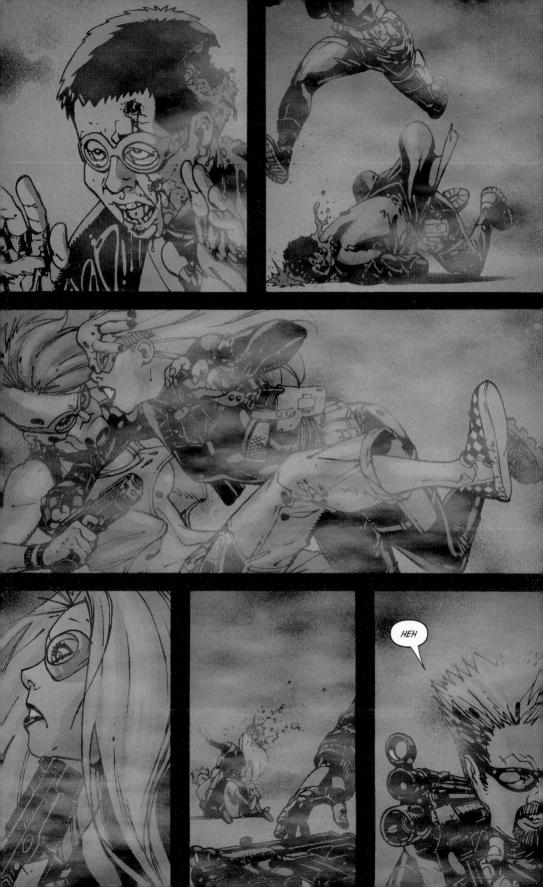

ILLUSTRATED BY
JASON PEARSON

COLORS BY
DAVID BARON
LETTERING BY
MICHAEL HEISLER
COVER BY
BRIAN WOOD
EDITED BY
SCOTT DUNBIER

CENTRAL IS SECURE.

AND I'VE GOT ONE WHO CAN TALK. WE ARE GOING TO FIND OUT EXACTLY WHO THEY WERE AND MAKE SURE THEY DON'T HURT ANYONE ELSE, EVER.

BECAUSE THAT'S WHAT THE GLOBAL FREQUENCY IS FOR.

CREATED AND WRITTEN BY
WARREN ELLIS

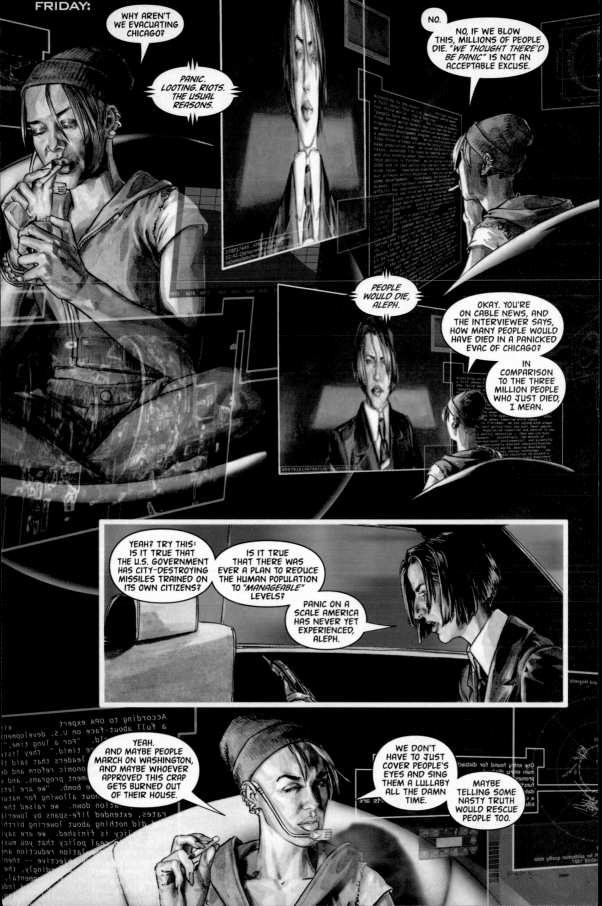

FRIDAY:

WHY AREN'T WE EVACUATING CHICAGO?

PANIC. LOOTING. RIOTS. THE USUAL REASONS.

NO. NO, IF WE BLOW THIS, MILLIONS OF PEOPLE DIE. "WE THOUGHT THERE'D BE PANIC" IS NOT AN ACCEPTABLE EXCUSE.

PEOPLE WOULD DIE, ALEPH.

OKAY. YOU'RE ON CABLE NEWS, AND THE INTERVIEWER SAYS, HOW MANY PEOPLE WOULD HAVE DIED IN A PANICKED EVAC OF CHICAGO?

IN COMPARISON TO THE THREE MILLION PEOPLE WHO JUST DIED, I MEAN.

YEAH? TRY THIS: IS IT TRUE THAT THE U.S. GOVERNMENT HAS CITY-DESTROYING MISSILES TRAINED ON ITS OWN CITIZENS?

IS IT TRUE THAT THERE WAS EVER A PLAN TO REDUCE THE HUMAN POPULATION TO "MANAGEABLE" LEVELS?

PANIC ON A SCALE AMERICA HAS NEVER YET EXPERIENCED, ALEPH.

YEAH. AND MAYBE PEOPLE MARCH ON WASHINGTON, AND MAYBE WHOEVER APPROVED THIS CRAP GETS BURNED OUT OF THEIR HOUSE.

WE DON'T HAVE TO JUST COVER PEOPLE'S EYES AND SING THEM A LULLABY ALL THE DAMN TIME.

MAYBE TELLING SOME NASTY TRUTH WOULD RESCUE PEOPLE TOO.

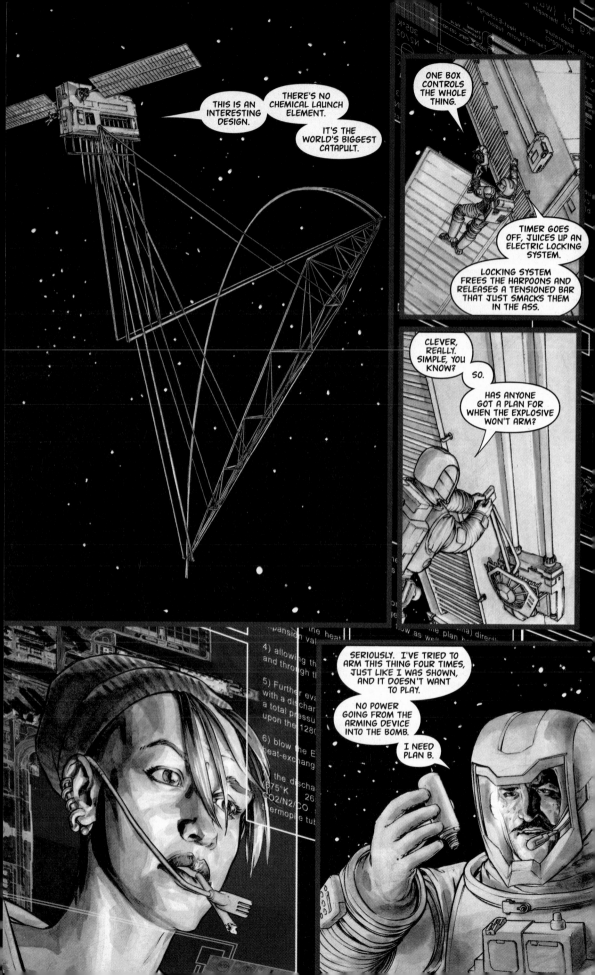

00:00:00.001

0:14:43.725

ARE YOU ON THE GLOBAL FREQUENCY?

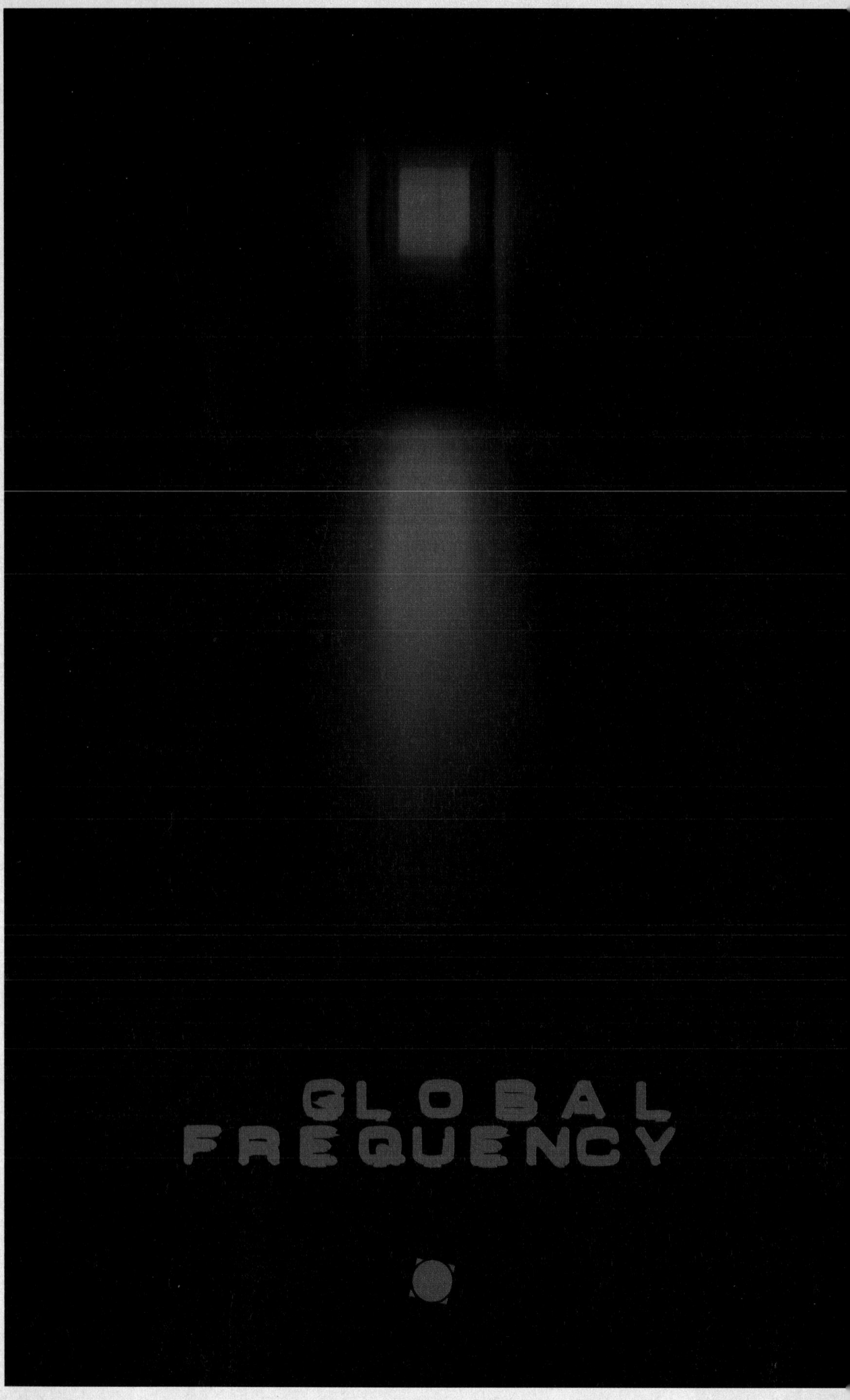
GLOBAL
FREQUENCY

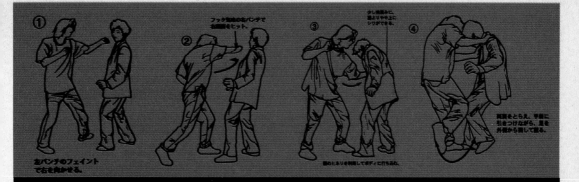

ARE YOU ON THE GLOBAL FREQUENCY?

ARE YOU ON THE **GLOBAL FREQUENCY**?

ARE YOU ON THE **GLOBAL FREQUENCY**?

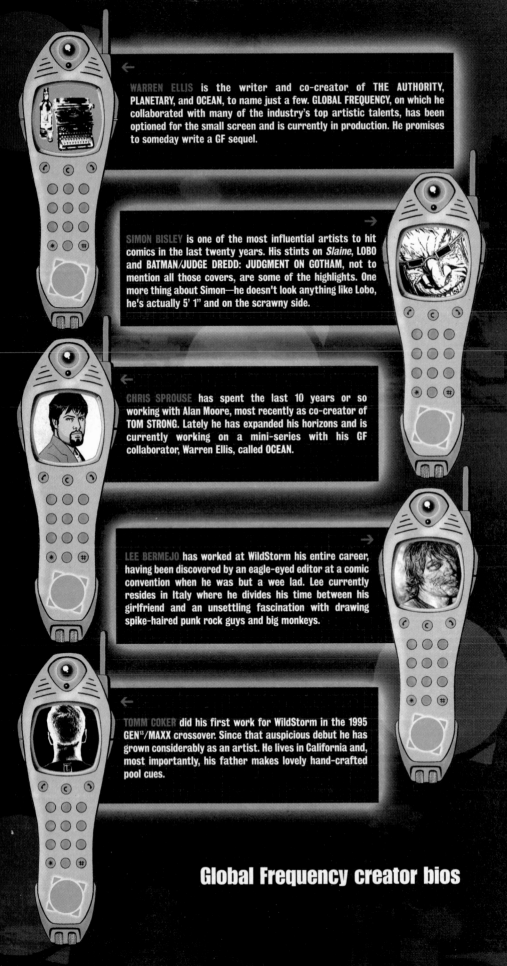

WARREN ELLIS is the writer and co-creator of THE AUTHORITY, PLANETARY, and OCEAN, to name just a few. GLOBAL FREQUENCY, on which he collaborated with many of the industry's top artistic talents, has been optioned for the small screen and is currently in production. He promises to someday write a GF sequel.

SIMON BISLEY is one of the most influential artists to hit comics in the last twenty years. His stints on *Slaine*, LOBO and BATMAN/JUDGE DREDD: JUDGMENT ON GOTHAM, not to mention all those covers, are some of the highlights. One more thing about Simon—he doesn't look anything like Lobo, he's actually 5' 1" and on the scrawny side.

CHRIS SPROUSE has spent the last 10 years or so working with Alan Moore, most recently as co-creator of TOM STRONG. Lately he has expanded his horizons and is currently working on a mini-series with his GF collaborator, Warren Ellis, called OCEAN.

LEE BERMEJO has worked at WildStorm his entire career, having been discovered by an eagle-eyed editor at a comic convention when he was but a wee lad. Lee currently resides in Italy where he divides his time between his girlfriend and an unsettling fascination with drawing spike-haired punk rock guys and big monkeys.

TOMM COKER did his first work for WildStorm in the 1995 GEN13/MAXX crossover. Since that auspicious debut he has grown considerably as an artist. He lives in California and, most importantly, his father makes lovely hand-crafted pool cues.

Global Frequency creator bios

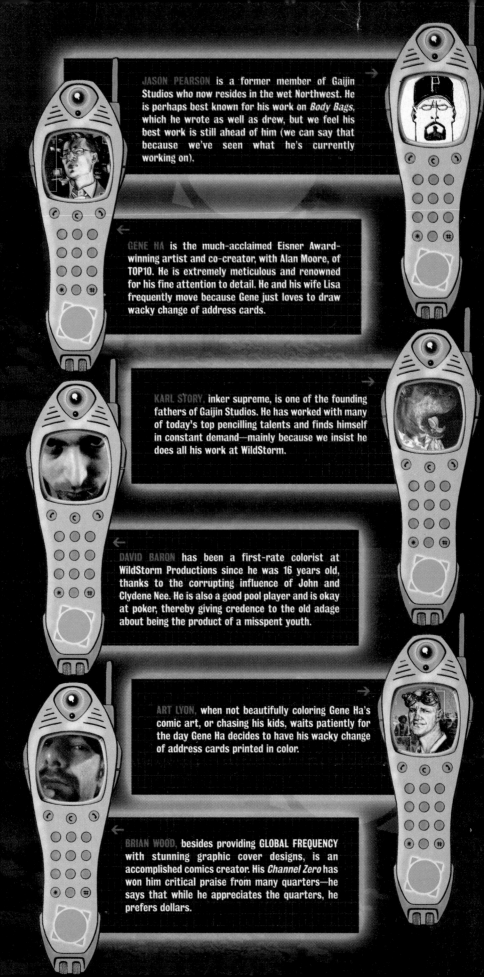

JASON PEARSON is a former member of Gaijin Studios who now resides in the wet Northwest. He is perhaps best known for his work on *Body Bags*, which he wrote as well as drew, but we feel his best work is still ahead of him (we can say that because we've seen what he's currently working on).

GENE HA is the much-acclaimed Eisner Award-winning artist and co-creator, with Alan Moore, of TOP10. He is extremely meticulous and renowned for his fine attention to detail. He and his wife Lisa frequently move because Gene just loves to draw wacky change of address cards.

KARL STORY, inker supreme, is one of the founding fathers of Gaijin Studios. He has worked with many of today's top pencilling talents and finds himself in constant demand—mainly because we insist he does all his work at WildStorm.

DAVID BARON has been a first-rate colorist at WildStorm Productions since he was 16 years old, thanks to the corrupting influence of John and Clydene Nee. He is also a good pool player and is okay at poker, thereby giving credence to the old adage about being the product of a misspent youth.

ART LYON, when not beautifully coloring Gene Ha's comic art, or chasing his kids, waits patiently for the day Gene Ha decides to have his wacky change of address cards printed in color.

BRIAN WOOD, besides providing GLOBAL FREQUENCY with stunning graphic cover designs, is an accomplished comics creator. His *Channel Zero* has won him critical praise from many quarters—he says that while he appreciates the quarters, he prefers dollars.

LOOK FOR THESE OTHER ABC/WILDSTORM BOOKS

**GLOBAL FREQUENCY:
PLANET ABLAZE**

ELLIS/VARIOUS

**BATMAN/DEATHBLOW:
AFTER THE FIRE**

AZZARELLO/BERMEJO

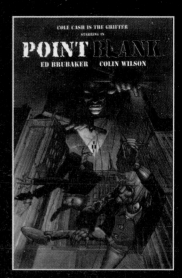

POINT BLANK

BRUBAKER/WILSON

**STORMWATCH:
TEAM ACHILLES
BOOKS 1 & 2**

WRIGHT/VARIOUS ARTISTS

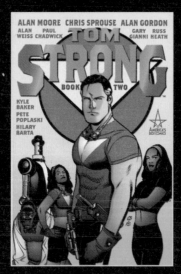

**TOM STRONG
BOOKS 1–3**

MOORE/SPROUSE/GORDON/STORY

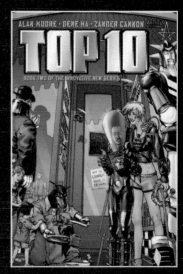

**TOP10
BOOKS 1 & 2**

MOORE/HA/CANNON

TO FIND MORE COLLECTED EDITIONS AND MONTHLY COMIC BOOKS FROM WILDSTORM AND DC COMICS, CALL 1-888-COMIC BOOK FOR THE NEAREST COMICS SHOP OR GO TO YOUR LOCAL BOOK STORE.